OH, THE THINGS A KHALA WILL DO

Written by Hanaa Unus
Illustrated by Stefano Pilia

Oh, the Things a Khala Will Do/ by Hanaa Unus
ISBN 10: 1490519432
ISBN 13: 9781490519432

Printed in the U.S.A

To my beloved
Zahra, Ibrahim, Bayan, and Rabia Senna,
And to my dear Ayyoob and Rumaysa
There are no words to fully express just how much
I love you.

Oh, the things a Khala will do to send you one message, "I love you!"

If it makes you laugh when you're sad, I'll "moo" just to show you that I love you.

I'll teach you about animals and take you to the zoo, just to show you that I love you.

I'll patiently wait in a long, long queue, just to show you that I love you.

Once in a while, I'll bring something new, just to show you that I love you.

I'll make you soup when you have the flu, just to show you that I love you.

I'll even pick up something that you threw, just to show you that I love you.

When something is lost, I'll give you a clue,
just to show you that I love you.

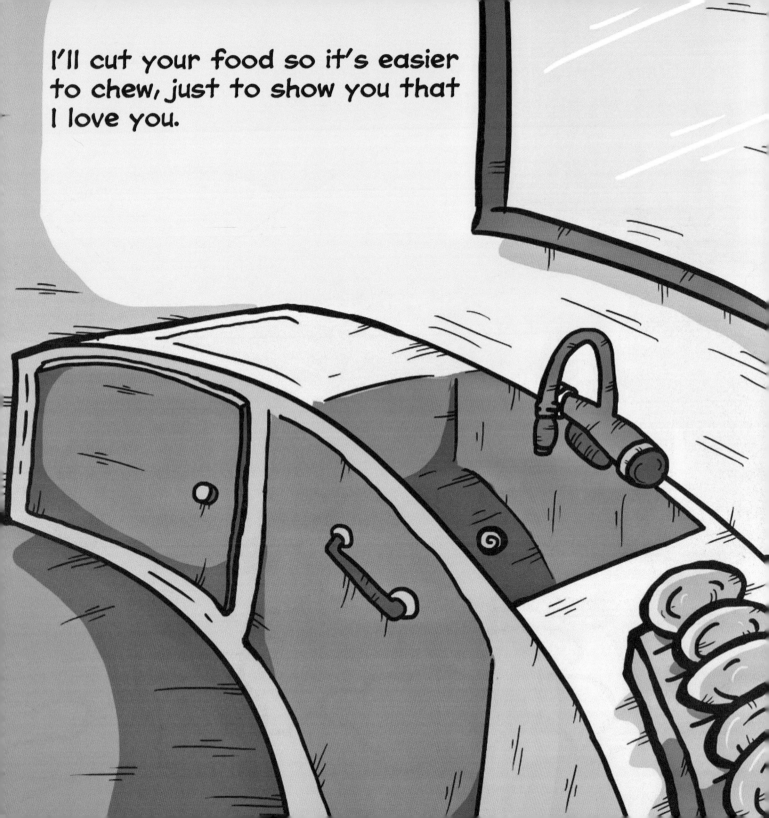

I'll help you with your shampoo,
just to show you that I love you.

When I have plans, I might cancel a few,
just to show you that I love you.

The truth is, I'd follow a kangaroo all the way to Kalamazoo, if it sent just this one message...

Printed in Great Britain
by Amazon

43925123R00021